River Otter's Adventure

by Linda Stanek

illustrated by Shennen Bersani

Baby otter shook the water from her fur, bounded up a mossy hill, and headed toward the zoo.

"I like being an otter, but
today I've decided to be . . .

"An elephant? Excuse me? Now, be gone!"

"Being an elephant was fun, but I think I'd miss the claws on my feet that diggity-dig in the riverbanks.

"So now I've decided to be . . .

"A naked mole rat? Ridiculous! Remove yourself."

"Being a naked mole rat was fun, but I think I'd miss my fuzzity-fluff fur that keeps me toasty in the winter, and dry while I splash and swim.

"So now I've decided to be . . .

"... a big, tundra musk ox!"

Musk Ox

WARM

WOOLY

COZY

SNUGGLY

"A musk ox? Outrageous! Now mosey on!"

"Being a musk ox was fun, but I think I'd miss my gurglety-slosh riverside home, where lunch waits just outside my door.

"So now I've decided to be . . .

"... a tiny, slippery salamander!"

Salamander

SQUISH

WIGGLE

SLURPING

JIGGLE

"A salamander? Simply silly! Now scat!"

"Being a salamander was fun, but I think I'd miss my squeakity-snort big loud voice that talks to others and calls out danger.

"So now I've decided to be . . .

"A gorilla? Gadzooks! Now get a move-on."

"Being a gorilla was fun, but I think I'd miss my muscley-strong tail that catapults me through the crystal water.

"So now I've decided to be . . .

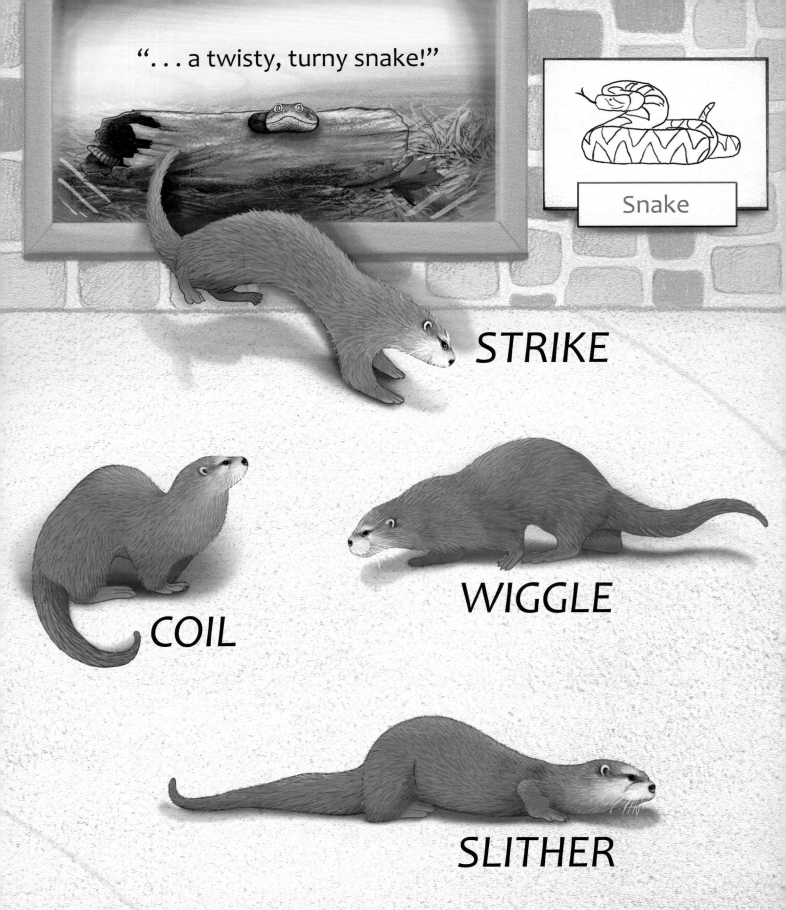

"A snake?" For heaven's sake! Now scoot!"

"Being a snake was fun, but I think I'd miss my twitchity-feel whiskers that help me find my way underwater.

"So now I've decided to be . . .

STALKING

ROAR!

SCREEEEEEE!

"Being a tiger was . . . SCARY, and right now
I'm missing so many ottery-life things."

Tiger

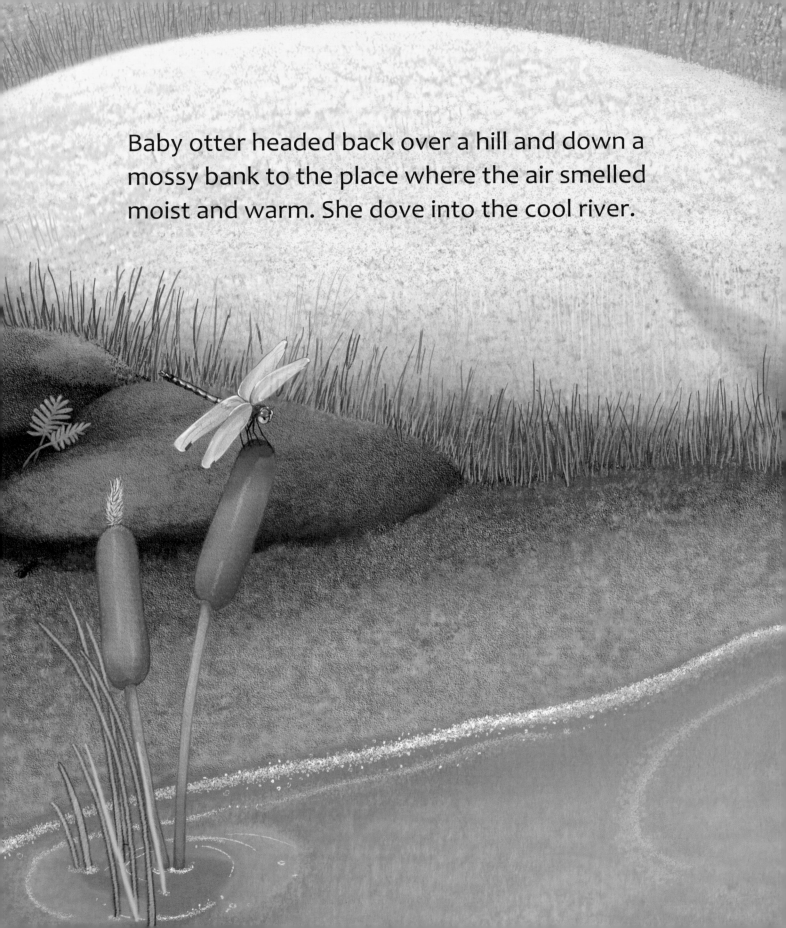

Baby otter headed back over a hill and down a mossy bank to the place where the air smelled moist and warm. She dove into the cool river.

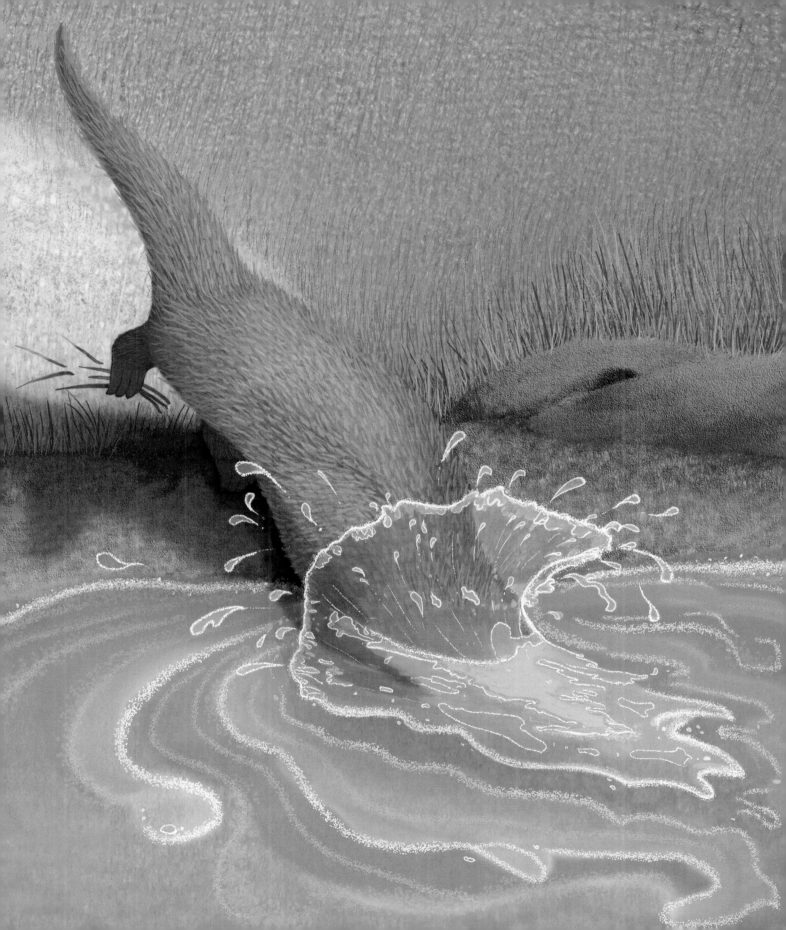

PLAY

SLIPPING

SPLASHING

DIVING

"So now I've decided to be . . .

"... a zippy, swimming, otter pup!

"ME!"

For Creative Minds

Basic Needs and Living and Nonliving Things

Like all living things, North American river otters have basic needs that must be met where they live. Basic needs include oxygen to breathe, water, food, and shelter from predators and the environment.

In all habitats and ecosystems, living things rely on both living things and nonliving things to survive. Can you identify which things found in a river otter's habitat are living and which are nonliving?

River otters live around **freshwater** rivers, streams and lakes, called the "riparian zone." Some even live around brackish (a mixture of salt and freshwater) salt marsh areas or coastlines. They cannot live in pure saltwater like the ocean but can "visit" pure saltwater areas. They move around well on land and in the water.

While these otters sometimes make their homes in abandoned beaver lodges or hollow trees, they usually dig a **den** in the soft **dirt** along a river bank and line it with grass, leaves, and fur. They build lots of tunnels to get in and out of their dens.

North American river otters mostly eat other **animals** but will also eat some **plants**. They eat almost any other small animals they find living near them including fish, crayfish, crabs, snails, turtles, frogs, insects, small rodents, birds, rabbits, ducks, and even snakes.

Like all mammals, river otters breathe **oxygen from the air**. If they are in the water, they come to the surface to breathe. If the water is frozen into ice during the winter, they make holes so they can come up to breathe. They can hold their breath for up to four minutes and can dive down 36 feet (11 meters).

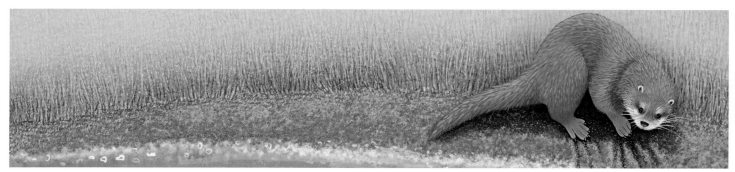

Answers: Basic Needs: Oxygen: air, water: fresh or brackish, food: most small animals found in their habitat and some plants but not trash, shelter: dens
Living things: animals and plants they eat, they line their dens with grass, leaves, and fur.
Nonliving things: freshwater, dirt, oxygen in air

North American River Otter or Sea Otter?

Many people get confused between North American river otters and sea otters.

Use the information in the chart to identify which images are North American river otters or sea otters.

A. B. C.

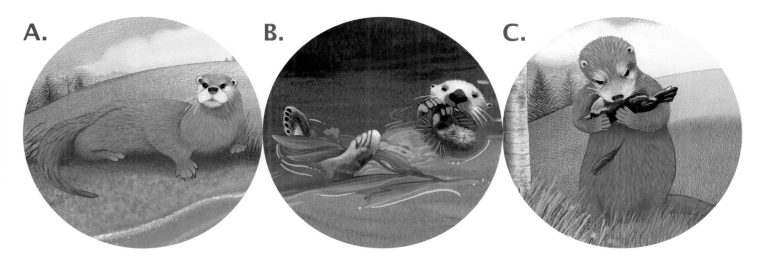

North American River Otter	Sea Otter
favorite foods: fish, crabs, frogs, crayfish, snails, rodents, birds	favorite foods: sea urchins, crabs, clams, shrimp, fish
usually eats on land	eats while floating on its back
swims with webbed feet	swims with hind feet and tail
swims belly down	floats on its back
gives birth on land	gives birth in the water
multiple pups born at a time	one single pup born at a time
lives in fresh or brackish water, will travel into salt water	lives in salt water
often comes on land and can move easily	rarely comes on land and is clumsy
rests in dens on land	rests in water, may wrap itself in kelp
main predators are alligators, bobcats, coyotes, wolves	main predators are orcas and sharks
lives all over the US and Canada	lives off the coasts in the North Pacific Ocean from California to Alaska and the east coast of Russia
one of 12 different river otter species found all over the world	only otter species that lives primarily in ocean (salt) water
member of the mustelid, or weasel, family	member of the mustelid, or weasel, family

Answers: A-river otter; B-sea otter; C-river otter

North American River Otter Adaptations

All animals have adaptations to help them live and survive in their habitat.

Some adaptations are parts of their bodies (physical).

Other adaptations are the way they do things (behavioral).

Can you figure out which of these adaptations are physical or behavioral?

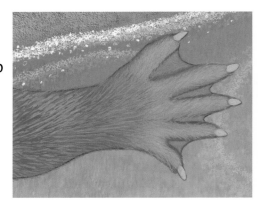

River otters have **claws** on their feet. These help otters grip in slippery mud or in snow or ice. Their claws also help them dig the tunnels that make their dens.

Otters' **webbed** feet help push them through the water, making them fast swimmers.

A river otter's **thick fur** keeps it warm. When swimming, a river otter's skin stays completely dry. That's because its fur catches air in it, keeping the water away from its skin. When a river otter swims, air bubbles escape from its fur, leaving a trail behind it.

River otters sometimes make a snorting **sound** to alert others to danger.

A frightened river otter can let out a scream that is so loud it carries a mile and a half over water.

Physical: claws & webbed feet; thick fur. Behavioral: making sounds

A river otter's **tail** is almost half of its total length. It's thick and muscular, and by swishing it, the otter pushes forward in the water.

River otters' flexible **spines** allow them to turn quickly and move with great speed in the water. They are so flexible that they sometimes swim in tight circles, creating whirlpools that bring their food to the surface for them.

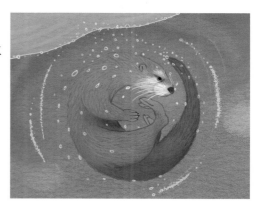

River Otters' thick **whiskers** help them feel around underwater.

River otters have a third, clear, **eyelid** called a nictitating membrane. It protects the otter's eye and allows it to see while swimming.

Not only that, their **eyes** can change shape underwater to help them focus.

River otters' **ears** and **nostrils** close tight to keep water out while they swim.

Physical: all of the above

To Rebecca, who believed in my writing before I did, and Allie, one of the great joys of my life. — LS

Dedicated to my grandson, Henry Manley. While doing the research for these illustrations Henry and I visited the North American river otters at the Stone Zoo, Stoneham, MA. I also visited the playful otters at Buttonwood Park Zoo, New Bedford; the Capron Park Zoo, North Attleboro; and the Blue Hills Trailside Museum, Milton; all in Massachusetts. Inspired by the otters swimming, I became a Red Cross certified lifeguard. — SB

Thanks to David Hamilton, General Curator at the Seneca Park Zoo and the North American River Otter Species Survival Plan Program Leader for the Association for Zoos and Aquariums for verifying the accuracy of the information in this book.

Library of Congress Cataloging-in-Publication Data

Names: Stanek, Linda, author. | Bersani, Shennen, illustrator.
Title: River otter's adventure / by Linda Stanek ; illustrated by Shennen Bersani.
Description: Mt. Pleasant : Arbordale Publishing, LLC, [2020] | Includes bibliographical references.
Identifiers: LCCN 2019057583 (print) | LCCN 2019057584 (ebook) | ISBN 9781643517568 (trade paperback) | ISBN 9781643517667 (pdf) | ISBN 9781643517766 (epub) | ISBN 9781643517865
Subjects: LCSH: Otters--Adaptation--Juvenile literature. | North American river otter--Juvenile literature. | Zoo animals--Juvenile literature. | Mimicry (Biology)--Juvenile literature.
Classification: LCC SF408.6.O74 S74 2020 (print) | LCC SF408.6.O74 (ebook) | DDC 639.97/9769--dc23
LC record available at https://lccn.loc.gov/2019057583
LC ebook record available at https://lccn.loc.gov/2019057584

Also available in Spanish paperback ISBN: 9781643517612 La aventura de la nutria de río

Keywords: adaptations, river otters

Bibliography/ Bibliografía:
BBC Wildlife Magazine. Discover Wildlife: Otters of the World. BBC Wildlife. Website. April, 2019.
Columbus Zoo Animal Guide: North American River Otter. Columbus Zoo and Aquarium. Web. Sept. 2017.
Katseanes, Sunny. "Re: teaching about river otters." Message to Linda Stanek. April 2019. Email.
North American River Otter. Birmingham Zoo. Web. Oct. 2017.
North American River Otter. Maryland Zoo. Web. Oct. 2017.
North American River Otter. National Geographic. Web. Sept. 2017.
North American River Otter. Smithsonian National Zoo and Conservation Biology Institute. Web. Oct. 2017.
North American River Otter. Utah's Hogle Zoo. Web. Oct. 2017.
Otter Specialist Group. International Union for Conservation of Nature and Natural Resources. Web. Oct. 2017.
What Are the Differences Between Sea Otters and River Otters? Seattle Aquarium. Web. April 2019.

Lexile® Level: 600L

Text Copyright 2020 © by Linda Stanek
Illustration Copyright 2020 © by Shennen Bersani

The "For Creative Minds" educational section may be copied by the owner for personal use or by educators using copies in classroom settings.

Printed in the U.S. August 2020
This product conforms to CPSIA 2008
First Printing

Arbordale Publishing
Mt. Pleasant, SC 29464
www.ArbordalePublishing.com